This Little Tiger book belongs to:

_____

_____ _____ _____

_____

For And - who first dreamt up Dinah -
flourish now and flourish ever!
- S P-H

For Elanur and Ediz
- R M

LITTLE TIGER
An imprint of Little Tiger Press Limited
1 Coda Studios, 189 Munster Road, London SW6 6AW
Imported into the EEA by Penguin Random House Ireland,
Morrison Chambers, 32 Nassau Street, Dublin D02 YH68
www.littletiger.co.uk

First published in Great Britain 2022
This edition published 2023

Text copyright © Smriti Prasadam-Halls 2022
Illustrations copyright © Richard Merritt 2022

Smriti Prasadam-Halls and Richard Merritt have asserted their rights
to be identified as the author and illustrator of this work under the
Copyright, Designs and Patents Act, 1988

A CIP catalogue record for this book is available from the British Library

FSC
www.fsc.org
MIX
Paper from
responsible sources
FSC® C017606

The Forest Stewardship Council® (FSC®) is an international,
non-governmental organisation dedicated to promoting responsible
management of the world's forests. FSC® operates a system of forest
certification and product labelling that allows consumers to identify
wood and wood-based products from well-managed forests.

For more information about the FSC®, please visit their website at www.fsc.org

DINOS DON'T GIVE UP!

Smriti Halls

Richard Merritt

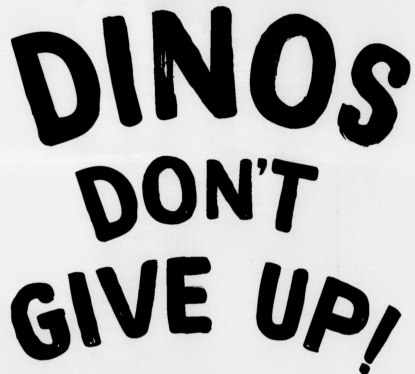

LiTTLE TiGER

LONDON

Once there was a dinosaur and Dinah was her name.
Known throughout the dino-world, she rose to dino fame.
In ALL the prehistoric land, no dino-tot was finer . . .
Than diplodocus darling,

little **dino Dinah!**

Dinah was a
superstar,

Dinah was a
WHIZZ,

When it came to - everything -
Dinah was the BIZ!

She'd build her blocks the highest
and she knew her A, B, C.

Letters, songs and numbers
all came *easy-peasily.*

Baking was a piece of cake,
ballet was a **breeze,**

Drawing was a doddle
and she mastered it with ease.

She never dropped a stitch
or got her knitting in a knot,

And when it came to archery,
she always hit the spot!

Dinah was an AWESOME pal,
she'd always lend a hand.

When friends found something difficult,
she'd help them understand.

She **CLAPPED** and **cheered** for everyone
– a friend so sweet and kind –
and even though she always won,
the others didn't mind.

Soon **every** little dinosaur
was racing up to try.

Dinah hadn't surfed before. How tricky could it be?
Take your board and stand on top –

like counting **1, 2, 3!**

DINOS, TAKE YOUR PLACES PLEASE. THE RACE WILL SOON BEGIN!

Dinah gave a dino-

stretch,

she knew she'd dino-win.

She wondered where she'd take her friends to celebrate her prize . . .
"DINO-SHAKES FOR ALL!" she thought. "An after-race SURPRISE!"

She gave a wave and took a bow, **quite** the surfing PRO.
The judges blew their whistles,

"Dinos!
Ready,
steady . . . GO!"

Dinah hopped aboard and yes,
she **tried** to surf the tide.

But she wibbled,
then she WOBBLED,

then she **swayed**
from side to side!

First she dino-**slipped** a bit
and then she dino-*slid*.

She couldn't stay afloat,
no matter **WHAT** she dino-did.

With a **flutter** in her tummy
and a **THUMPING** in her chest,
She got the sinking feeling that
she might not be the best!

She didn't have the skill at all,
oh how she dino-knew it.
She wasn't going to win this race!

She couldn't
dino-do-it!

Clinging to her surfboard,
she made one more desperate dash,
But everything was over
in a single frantic **flash** . . .

SPLASH!

Each and every surfer
soon went bobbing, gliding past.
And for the first time EVER
dino Dinah ended . . .

...last!

Dinah's eyes filled up with tears!
Oh **what** a dino-muddle!

But her friends knew what she needed most . . .

. . . a
GREAT big
dino-cuddle.

Feeling SO much better,
Dinah gave her bravest smile.
"Well done!" she told the winner,
"**WOW!** I really like your style!"

She cheered for all her friends
and said, "I know I didn't win.
But I think surfing's loads of fun . . .
Come on! Who's coming in?"

With that, she grabbed her surfboard, took a DEEP breath, smiled, and then . . .
Summoned all her **COURAGE** . . . and jumped back on her board again!

Yes, Dinah and her friends showed how it's **REALLY** dino-done . . .

By picking yourself up again and simply having fun.

More **inspiring** books from Little Tiger . . .

NEVER MESS WITH A PIRATE PRINCESS
Holly Ryan
Siân Roberts

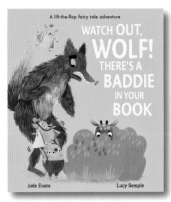

Dream Big Little One
Becky Davies
Dana Brown

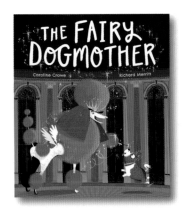

THE FAIRY DOGMOTHER
Caroline Crowe
Richard Merritt

HOW TO MAKE A BOOK
Becky Davies
Patricia Ho

A lift-the-flap fairy tale adventure
WATCH OUT, WOLF! THERE'S A BADDIE IN YOUR BOOK
Jude Evans
Lucy Semple

IMPOSSIBLE!
Tracey Corderoy
Tony Neal

LITTLE TIGER

For information regarding any of the above titles or for our catalogue,
please contact us: Little Tiger Press Limited,
1 Coda Studios, 189 Munster Road, London SW6 6AW
Tel: 020 7385 6333 • Email: contact@littletiger.co.uk • www.littletiger.co.uk